MAGGIE

SPARKS

AND THE
MONSTER
BABY

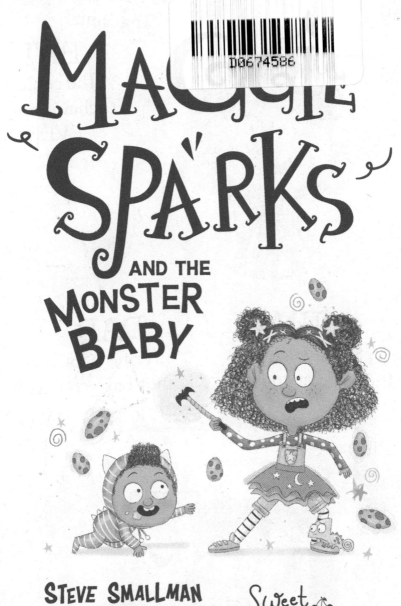

STEVE SMALLMAN

ILLUSTRATED BY
ESTHER HERNANDO

Sweet
Cherry

MAGGIE
That's me!

BAT
The coolest
chameleon
EVER.

MUM
Super smart.
Bakes great cookies.

DAD
Writes a lot.
Cannot bake cookies.

ALFIE
Stinky and annoying.

GRANDAD
My favourite
wizard in the world!

ARTHUR
My best friend.

CHAPTER 1

Maggie Sparks was a witch. A small, curly-haired, freckle-faced witch, who was usually full of mischief and fizzing with

MAGIC.

But not today. Today she was worried.

Grandad Sparks, Maggie's favourite person in the whole world, was looking after her while Mum and Dad were away. She should have been as happy as a witch who'd worked out the secret to an excellent slime spell. But she wasn't.

Grandad could see that Maggie was worried. Even Bat, her pet chameleon, had changed colour to Worry White to match Maggie's mood.

'Don't worry,' said Grandad Sparks. 'Mummy and Daddy will be home soon!'

'That's what I'm worried about!' cried Maggie.

Mum and Dad had gone to the hospital to swap Mum's big tummy for a baby. They'd been gone for AAAAAAAAGES.

'What do they want a baby for?' said Maggie. 'What's the matter with me?'

'There's nothing the matter with you, Maggie Moo!' said Grandad Sparks. He gave her one of his warm, crinkly smiles. 'But think what fun it will be to have a baby brother!'

'Can't I have a goldfish instead?' asked Maggie.

'Well, no,' said Grandad Sparks.

'But you'll be able to play with your brother.'

'I could *play* with a goldfish,' said Maggie.

'Yes, but one day,' Grandad Sparks went on, 'you'll be able to do *magic* with your brother!'

Maggie's eyes lit up.

'I can do magic on the baby?' she said with a grin. 'Brilliant! I could turn him into a goldfish!'

'No, no, not *on* him, *with* him!' said Grandad Sparks.

'That's boring,' grumbled Maggie.

'Just you wait, Maggie. As soon as you see him, you'll love him to bits.'

Suddenly, a terrible screeching noise came from outside.

Was it a terrifying pterodactyl pouncing on Penny the postwoman? Was it a tomcat with his tail trapped in a toilet seat?

No. It was Maggie's new baby brother.

Bat dived into the fruit bowl and disguised himself as a banana.

Seconds later, Mum and Dad marched through the door. They were smiling proudly and holding a screaming bundle.

'Look Maggie!' Dad shouted over the noise. 'This is Alfie!'

Maggie looked down at the little noise monster. Its face was all red and wrinkly. It had no hair, no teeth and was covered in dribble. **YUCK!**

'What a beautiful baby boy!' said Grandad Sparks.

'Beautiful?' said Maggie. 'He looks like an angry turnip! Why is he making that noise?'

'He's just hungry,' said Mum. She popped a bottle into Alfie's mouth.

As if by magic, the noise stopped.
'Is that magic milk?' asked Maggie.

'No,' chuckled Dad. 'It's Mummy milk.'

Mummy milk? Maggie was confused. 'But I thought milk only came from–'

'Cows?' suggested Dad.

'Fridges,' said Maggie.

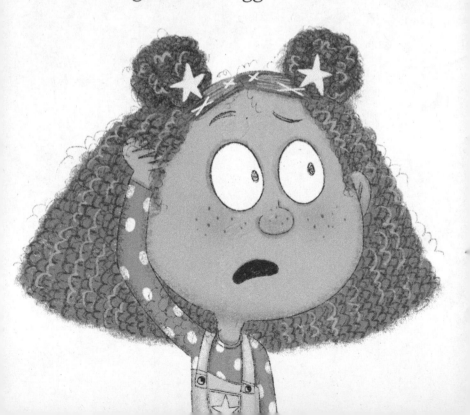

Then Dad propped Alfie over
his shoulder, patted his back and ...

BURRRRRP!

'Good boy!'
said Mum.

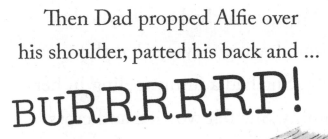

Maggie watched as everybody gazed down gooey-eyed at the baby. She had a funny feeling in her tummy. She felt worried and cross and sad all at the same time.

Bat turned bright green.

OH DEAR!

Maggie wasn't just worried and cross and sad, she was jealous too.

Bat could sense Maggie's magic was building. Her fingers began to tingle and tiny sparks started to fizz from her hair. Bat ducked further down into the fruit bowl.

Turning away from Mum and
Dad, Maggie reached up her sleeve
and pulled out her wand. She could
make a much bigger burp than
snotty baby Alfie. All she needed
was a little MAGIC.

Maggie wiggled her wand and
whispered:

'Wild wind blow
and thunder roar,
make my burp better
than the one before!'

There was a short pause before,

'BUUUURRRRRRP!'

The curtains flapped. The
floorboards rattled. The awful picture
of Great Auntie Enid fell on the
floor and Grandad Sparks's hat blew
right off his head!

It was the biggest burp that
Maggie had ever burped. She waited
to be told 'Good girl!' and maybe
even get a round of applause.

'Maggie!' gasped Dad.

'That was very rude!' said Mum.

The monster baby
started crying again.

Grandad Sparks
just shook his
head and picked
up his hat.

Maggie sat scowling in the
"naughty corner", while Mum
rocked Alfie to sleep on the sofa.
Bat climbed onto Maggie's shoulder
and licked her ear. It usually made
her laugh. But not today.

Maggie looked over her shoulder
at the tiny monster, now fast asleep
in *her* mum's arms.

'Maggie?' said Mum. 'Would you
like to hold Alfie? You can come out
of the naughty corner and sit next

31

to me,' she added, patting the sofa cushion next to her.

'No,' snapped Maggie. 'I think he should go in his cage now.'

'It's a cot, Maggie, not a cage,' said Mum, as she stood up and laid the sleeping baby inside it.

'Well, I think I'd better leave you to it,' said Grandad Sparks, heaving himself up off the sofa.

He kissed Mum, hugged Dad and stroked the monster's little head. Then he picked Maggie up and gave her a big cuddle.

'See you later, Maggie Moo,' he said. Then he whispered in her ear,

'Brilliant burp!'

Maggie smiled and started to feel a bit happier.

The baby was behind bars (where it belonged!) and Mum had freed Maggie from the "naughty corner" a whole three minutes early.

Maggie looked at Alfie through the side of his cot. He looked less like a turnip now. He was even smiling in his sleep. Maggie could feel the corners of her mouth start to curl up just a tiny bit before a loud

PARP

came from his nappy.

'Ew! We'll have to keep an eye on this one,' Maggie whispered to Bat. 'He's trouble!'

CHAPTER 2

Maggie had been right. Alfie *was* trouble. Things only got worse as he got bigger!

At first, he'd stayed where he was put: in his cot or on his blanket. But once the drooling monster learnt to crawl and climb and pull himself up onto the furniture, nothing was safe. Maggie had to magic her things up onto the ceiling so he

couldn't reach them. But
after a while they all came
tumbling back down again.
Then she got
told off for
making a mess.
But when
Alfie made a
mess, Mum and
Dad laughed. He
pooed in his pants and
they didn't seem to care.

He threw his breakfast on the floor,
blew raspberries at the dinner table,
chewed books and could empty a
tissue box in less than a minute.
But he never got told off!

IT WAS SOOOOOOO
UNFAIR!

Alfie even got to stay up late with Mum and Dad when Maggie was sent to bed. Everyone thought he was so wonderful. Everyone except Maggie.

One morning,
Mum and Maggie were
walking down the hill into
town. Maggie was pushing
Alfie's buggy. She was just
thinking how much faster the
buggy would get to the bottom of
the hill if she let go of it, when they
bumped into Penny the postwoman.

As usual, Penny looked like she
was going to start complaining
about something. Then she suddenly
spotted Alfie and smiled. 'Oh, what a
lovely little fella!' she said.

Later, in Mum's flower shop,
Mr Battenberg from the bakery
saw Alfie through the window and
rushed in just to see him.

'Oh, aren't you adorable!' he cooed.
Then he looked around, realised
where he was and added, 'I'll have
two bunches of daffodils since I'm
here, please Hetty!'

It was just as bad at the
supermarket! An old lady leant
over, poked Alfie's tummy
with her knobbly finger
and said, 'Who's this
widdle dumply
wumply woo, then?'

Yes, everyone loved Alfie. And nobody seemed to notice Maggie at all.

Maggie started to feel strange.

Her toes began to tingle as they trudged back up the hill to their house. By the time they reached their garden gate, Maggie's feet felt so itchy that she pulled down her socks to scratch them.

But her feet had disappeared!

'MUM!' she cried. 'MY FEET!'

'Yes, I know,' said Mum, as she tried to stop Alfie from biting a hole in a box of coco puffs. 'My feet are aching too. That hill seems to be getting steeper every day!'

'BUT MUM!'

Maggie tried again. She was interrupted by a loud squelching sound coming from the bottom end of Alfie. It was followed by a smell so bad it made Maggie's eyes water.

Mum carried Alfie into the house at arm's length to change his nappy.

Maggie sighed and went up to her room. She took off her shoes and socks. Oh no! Her feet really had disappeared. Then she lifted up her T-shirt. Oh dear! Her tummy wasn't there either. And now her arms were fading away too.

Maggie shut the door and quickly took off her clothes. She looked in the mirror and nearly fell over onto her invisible bottom.

Only her head was left! It looked as if it were floating in mid-air!

Then, as she watched, her face
went fuzzy around the edges. It
started to lose colour and then,
suddenly, it disappeared altogether.

'Oh no!' Maggie cried. 'I really am
invisible!'

The shouting woke Bat, who had
been dozing on his sleeping stick
beside Maggie's bed.

'Oh Bat,' Maggie said. 'What am I going to do?'

Bat looked all around the room, which didn't take long because he could look in two directions at once. He could hear Maggie, but he definitely couldn't see her. Maggie sniffed and wiped a tear from her eye. 'How am I going to comb my hair?' she said. 'Or clean my teeth? Or do my homework?'

Then she remembered that she didn't like combing her hair or cleaning her teeth or doing her homework.

'If nobody can see me,' Maggie said, 'then nobody can see what I'm doing. Oh, this could be fun!'

Maggie fetched a white sheet from the cupboard and pulled it over her head. Then she tiptoed across the landing to Dad's office.

She pushed the door open and let out a loud,

'WOOOOOOOOOOOH!'

Dad nearly fell off his chair. His arm shot to the side and knocked a mug of coffee all over his desk.

'Maggie!' he said crossly. 'I'm trying to work!' He walked across the room and snatched the sheet from her head.

But when he saw that there was nothing underneath the sheet, Dad's face turned very pale.

He gave a little squeak, dropped the sheet and ran downstairs.

'Are you alright, dear?' asked Mum. 'You look like you've seen a ghost!'

'Just need t-t-to pop to the doctors,' he said, rubbing his forehead. 'N-n-nothing to worry about, darling.' Then he unlocked the door and walked quickly down the road, muttering to himself, 'I must be seeing things. And hearing things. Maybe it's hunger. Or too much coffee. I *need* to cut down on the coffee.'

Maggie was trying really hard not to giggle as she tiptoed down the stairs.

A lovely sweet, chocolatey smell was coming from the kitchen.

Alfie was strapped into his high chair and Mum was loading the dishwasher. A tray full of double chocolate chip cookies were cooling on the table. Alfie was stretching his chubby little hands out to reach them, but Mum had made sure his high chair was too far away.

This was Maggie's chance. She stepped silently towards the table. She was only going to take a couple. But, wait … she had a brilliant idea!

What if Alfie stole the cookies? That would show Mum what the little monster was really like. Very quietly and verrrrrry slowly, Maggie pushed Alfie's high chair closer to the cookies.

With a squeal of delight, the
dribbly demon grabbed the corner of
the tray and flipped all the cookies
into the air.

'Alfie, no!' cried Mum, as cookies went everywhere.

Mum was so busy clearing up that she didn't notice when three cookies floated out of the door.

'YUM!' said Maggie, as she stood in the hallway scoffing down the chocolate chip goodies.

She felt very pleased with herself.

'Oh Alfie,' said Mum, sadly. 'I made these cookies especially for Maggie, to cheer her up. Now they are all over the floor.'

Maggie felt awful. Mum had been doing something nice, just for her!

Maggie started to feel warm all over. The more she felt

as though she mattered, the more
visible she became. First her head
appeared, then her shoulders, her
tummy, her arms, her legs, her fingers
and finally her ten little toes appeared
like two rows of magic beans.

'I'm back!' said Maggie.

'Maggie!' cried Mum, looking
out into the hallway. 'What are you
doing? Why haven't you got any
clothes on?'

Maggie didn't
know what to say.
She turned and ran
back to her bedroom
to find some clothes.

CHAPTER 3

Maggie had just got dressed again
when–

DING DONG!

She rushed downstairs to see who
was at the door.

A small, scruffy-haired boy wearing
glasses and a duffle coat that was too
big for him stood on the doorstep.

It was Maggie's best friend, Arthur.

Arthur wasn't a wizard or anything.

It's fair to say that there was
nothing magical about Arthur.

Right then he was staring at the
ground, looking worried. But then
Arthur usually looked worried.
He had a worried sort of face.

'Hello, Arthur. You will never believe the day I've had today!' said Maggie. 'And it's all because of that little monster!'

'What little monster?' asked Arthur, looking around nervously.

Arthur never knew what to expect at Maggie's house. There could be a dragon in the dining room, a bogeyman in the bathroom or a troll in the toilet for all he knew! **'THAT MONSTER!'** said Maggie as Alfie crawled into the hall.

Alfie looked up at Arthur, giggled and gave him a great big, two-toothed

smile! Arthur smiled back at
him, gave a little wave and said,
'Hello Alfie!' in a silly, sing-
song voice.

Maggie couldn't
believe it!

'You traitor!' she shouted. 'You're supposed to be my friend! But with one smile from that little pest, you go all smiley and gooey.'

'But he's soooooooooo cute,' said Arthur. 'Even if he is a pest. He's like a mouse.'

'What are you talking about?' asked Maggie.

'Well,' said Arthur, 'some people think mice are pests, but some people think they're cute. I like mice, but not if they poo in your lunchbox. My uncle Norman had a mouse that pooed in his lunch box once. He had a piece of chocolate cake in it and he thought the mouse poo was a bit of chocolate, so he ate it. But it didn't taste like chocolate, it tasted like mouse poo.'

Maggie rolled her eyes.

'Goodbye Arthur,' she said and closed the door.

'Er ... I'll be going then,' Arthur shouted through the letter box. Then he shuffled back down the garden path.

Maggie stomped up to her bedroom and slammed the door.

Arthur had been no help and more annoyingly, he was right. Alfie was so stupidly cute!

'That's why he gets away with so much!' she told Bat. 'He just has to flash a smile, pull a funny face or put a potty on his head and everyone melts.

'Oh, Bat,' she sighed. 'I must make myself cuter. Even cuter than a mouse who hasn't done a poo in a lunch box!'

Maggie looked at herself in the mirror.

'What if I pull out my teeth?' she said. 'Alfie only has two teeth. Would

I look cuter with just two teeth?'

Bat shook his head in panic.

'Hmm,' Maggie said, opening her pyjama drawer. 'I could start wearing pyjamas all the time. And nappies. Maybe I should rub yoghurt all over my face?'

Bat shook his head again.

'Well if that will not work, then
I suppose it's time for a little bit of
magic!'

Maggie searched under the piles of clothes, toys and books scattered around her room.

'Bat, have you seen my wand?' she asked, with a stray sock draped over one ear.

Bat crossed his fingers behind his back and shook his head.

'Bat, did you hide my wand again?'

The chameleon blushed and looked down at his feet. Then he crawled under the bed.

There, in a jumble of colouring pencils,

half-eaten biscuits and spilt potions,
lay Maggie's wand. It was short,
stripy, slightly bent and had a bat-
shaped rubber stuck on the end.

Bat used his tail to pass the wand
to Maggie, then quickly dived back
under the bed.

Maggie wiggled her wand and
chanted:

'Sweet as ice cream
on a big bowl of fruit,
magic please make me
incredibly cute!'

POOF!

Maggie looked in the mirror and there, staring back at her, was a soft, floppy-eared bunny rabbit, with big brown eyes and a little pink heart-shaped nose.

'Noooooooo!' Maggie said – or tried to say. But no words came out.

This was not what she had meant!

She needed to cast another spell to fix this one. But she couldn't pick up her wand with her bunny paws. She couldn't say the words of a spell either, because she could only speak bunny (and bunnies hardly speak at all!).

I'll find Mum, thought Maggie. *Maybe she can help.*

Maggie jumped up at the door handle. After five tries, she managed to open the door. She hopped clumsily down the stairs with a worried little chameleon scuttling after her.

Maggie could hear Mum
talking on the phone. She
hopped towards the living
room. But before she got there
Alfie came crawling out into the hall.

'BUM BUM!' he said excitedly,
and tried to grab Maggie by her
fluffy tail.

Maggie jumped this way and that but she hadn't had much hopping practice, and Alfie could crawl at lightning speed. He grabbed Maggie and gave her a big squeeze.

'Aah,' Alfie cooed.

Maggie tried to shout, 'Get off!' But all that came out was a squeak.

Bat bravely darted forwards, stuck out his long tongue and tickled Alfie's ear with it. Alfie giggled, dropped Maggie and grabbed Bat instead!

Alfie gave Bat a big squeeze. Bat's tongue shot out and his curly tail straightened like a party blower. Alfie giggled. He was having a great time. Bat was not.

Thankfully, the front door opened, distracting the chameleon-squeezing monster.

'I'm home,' said Dad, peeking around the door to check for imaginary ghosts. 'Ok, no ghosts, that's good,' he said, letting out a deep breath.

'Da-da?' said Alfie and dropped Bat on the floor.

Maggie hopped over to rescue Bat, who jumped onto her back like a cowboy.

'Bum bum!' cried Alfie, reaching for Maggie again. But with one mighty hop, Maggie shot towards Dad, slid through his legs and tumbled straight out of the front door.

Without even noticing
the flying bunny, Dad scooped
Alfie up one-handed and closed
the door with his foot.

SLAM!

Maggie and Bat were
locked out.

CHAPTER 4

Alfie started to cry.

'Bum bum!' he wailed.

'What's wrong with Alfie?' asked Dad. 'Why does he keep shouting about his bum?'

'Oh!' said Mum, coming out into the hallway. 'What a clever little sausage! I expect he wants you to change his nappy. It seems you got home just in time.'

Dad grumbled.

But even after his nappy had been changed, Alfie kept on crying. 'Bum bum! BUM BUM!'

Dad handed him back to Mum. 'Where's Maggie?' he asked.

'Upstairs in her room,' said Mum. 'She hasn't been herself today. She was running around earlier with no clothes on!'

'Maggie?' Dad called, running up the stairs. 'Where's my little girl?' He opened her bedroom door. Of course, Maggie wasn't there.

And she wasn't a little girl, either. At that moment, Maggie was a

floppy-eared bunny rabbit with a
chameleon on her back. And she
was galloping, flippity floppity down

the street with a large, slobbery dog snapping at her heels!

The dog was called Rufus. He had always been her friend when she was Maggie the witch. But now that she was Maggie the bunny, he seemed determined to gobble her up!

Maggie didn't know which way
to turn and was about to dash out
into the road when Bat decided to
take control. He grabbed Maggie's
long ears and used them to steer
her. He pulled her left ear to avoid
a passing cyclist, and her right ear

to steer around a pile of dog poo.
Then, suddenly, he pulled both ears
together. Maggie skidded to a stop
right next to a small gap in the fence.
They dived through it just in time!

Rufus was too big to get through
the gap. He was left behind, barking

furiously, as Maggie and Bat ran off across the park and into the woods beyond.

Maggie and Bat flopped down, panting on the leafy ground. They looked around them. It was very dark under the trees and they could hear something moving in the bushes. What if it was a hungry fox who fancied a bunny for dinner and a chameleon for dessert?

Maggie gulped. She didn't know what to do. She was cold, tired, sad, scared and lost. Bat didn't know which colour to change to first!

Then it started to rain.

Maggie's floppy ears drooped, her pink nose twitched and big bunny teardrops splashed onto Bat, who was now clinging to her furry tummy.

Suddenly, in the distance, they saw a tiny light glowing in the dark.

Maggie made a noise that sounded like a squeak, but was probably 'Eek! It's a fox! A fox with one eye!' in rabbit language.

But it wasn't a hungry one-eyed fox. It was a firefly.

Then there was another and another, until the woods were speckled with hundreds of magical fireflies lighting a path.

Bat thought that the fireflies
looked rather tasty and caught two
or three with his long tongue as they
hopped deeper into the woods.

Following the glowing path,
Maggie and Bat arrived at a clearing
where a lopsided building huddled
under the trees. It had a tower on
one side, a rather wonky chimney
on the other, and soft orangey light
shining from its windows.

Maggie beamed a big bunny smile.
It was Grandad Sparks's cottage! She
hurried to the door and scratched
at it with her claws. Bat climbed
up and dangled from the doorbell,

making it ring over
and over again.

Back at home, Mum and Dad were worried. They had looked everywhere for Maggie: behind the sofa, under the table, in the shower, on top of the wardrobe, even under the sink.

'Maggie, where are you?' called Mum in a panic.

'Hetty! In here! Quick!' called Dad from Maggie's bedroom. 'Look, it's Maggie's wand.'

'Oh no!' cried Mum. 'What if Maggie's been doing magic? Anything could have happened!'

'We'd better go and look for her!' said Dad, strapping Alfie to his chest

96

in a baby sling. Alfie was still crying, but as soon as they went outside, he stopped.

'BUM BUM!' he shouted.

CHAPTER 5

Grandad Sparks
opened his cottage
door and was surprised
to see Maggie's
chameleon hanging
from his doorbell.

'Hello little fellow!'
he said. 'What are you
doing here? Where's
Maggie?'

Bat pointed his tail at the doorstep. Grandad Sparks looked down to see a rather soggy bunny looking back at him.

'Oh dear! Is that you, Maggie Moo?'

The bunny nodded.

'Well come on in before you catch a cold!' said Grandad Sparks, hurrying them both inside.

He dried Maggie and Bat with warm towels, wrapped them up in blankets and sat them by the fire. As they sat warming their toes, Grandad Sparks rang Maggie's dad.

'Sorry, I can't talk now,' said Dad.
'We can't find Maggie and we think
she's been doing magic! We've
looked all over but there's no sign—'

'She's here!' said Grandad Sparks.
'Bat's here too.'

'OH, THANK GOODNESS!'
gasped Dad.

Then Mum grabbed the phone,

'IS SHE ALRIGHT?'

'Er, well, she seems OK, but she's a bit ...'

'A bit what?' asked Mum.

'A bit ... fluffier than usual,' said Grandad Sparks.

A few minutes later, Mum and Dad burst through the door of Grandad Sparks's cottage. They couldn't believe their eyes!

Mum knelt down and gently stroked the soft fur behind Maggie's ears. 'Oh, Maggie, why did you turn yourself into a bunny?'

'Bum bum!' cried Alfie, trying to wriggle out of his baby sling to reach Maggie.

'Oh!' laughed Dad. 'He didn't want me to change his nappy at all. He was trying to say "bunny"!'

'Never mind changing nappies,' said Grandad Sparks. 'How do we change Maggie back into a little girl?'

'I could try a spell?' said Dad.

'Are you sure, Tom?' asked Mum in a worried voice.

'Of course!' he said, handing her a dribble-covered Alfie. 'But I'll need a bit more light!'

Dad pointed his wand at the light bulb and said:

'Sunshine gold
and lightning white,
give us lots
of lovely light!'

POOF!

The spell worked! The light bulb grew brighter and brighter and brighter ...

'That's enough darling,' said Mum.

But Dad didn't know how to stop the spell. Suddenly ...

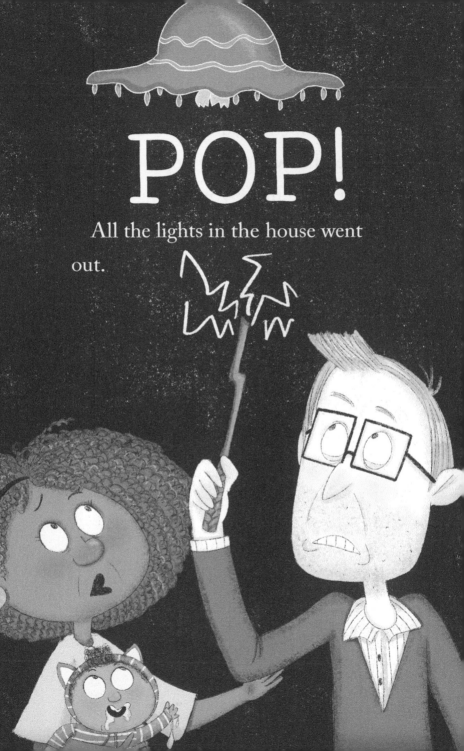

POP!

All the lights in the house went out.

Dad jumped in surprise and
dropped his wand. 'Whoops!'

'You are definitely *not* doing any
spells on Maggie,' said Mum firmly.

The room was dark now, except for
the glow from the fire and an extra
glow coming from Bat's tummy.

'Hmm,' said Grandad Sparks,
as he reached into the cupboard
for some candles. 'It looks like
someone's been eating my fireflies.'

Grandad Sparks lit
the candles and soon the
room was flickering with
bright golden light.

Grandad Sparks, Mum and Dad huddled together and talked in whispers (the way grown-ups do when they don't want children to hear what they're saying).

But while the adults were whispering, Alfie was crawling towards Maggie ... holding Dad's wand! Alfie sat down beside Maggie, reached out his sticky little hands and gave her a big hug.

'Bye, bye, bum bum,' he said.

POOF!

Maggie turned back into a little girl. She had human hands and

human toes and curly human hair
again.

Maggie was so happy to be back to
normal that she hugged Alfie back.

Mum and Dad and Grandad Sparks rushed over, freed Dad's wand from Alfie's sticky fingers and pulled him and Maggie into a great big group hug.

For the first time in a long time, Maggie felt happy and special and loved. Bat turned a bright, sunshine yellow.

Maybe, thought Maggie, having a baby brother isn't so bad.

PAAAAAAAARP!

Maggie's eyes started watering. 'Ew! Alfieeeee!'

Continue the magic in ...

MAGGIE SPARKS

AND THE SWIMMING POOL SHARKS